This rising moon book

belongs to

Because You Are My Baby

by Jennifer Ward
illustrations by Sylvia Long

rising moon

www.risingmoonbooks.com

Composed in the United States of America
Printed in China

Edited by Theresa Howell
Designed by Sunny H. Yang

FIRST IMPRESSION 2007
ISBN 13: 978-0-87358-911-6
ISBN 10: 0-87358-911-4

07 08 09 10 11 5 4 3 2 1

Library of Congress Cataloging-in-Publication Data

Ward, Jennifer, 1963-
Because you are my baby / by Jennifer Ward ; illustrated by Sylvia Long.
p. cm.
Summary: Rhyming text explores the ways different animals care for their offspring, from roadrunners to skunks to humans.
ISBN-13: 978-0-87358-911-6 (hardcover)
ISBN-10: 0-87358-911-4 (hardcover)
[1. Parental behavior in animals--Fiction. 2. Parent and child--Fiction. 3. Animals--Fiction. 4. Stories in rhyme.] I. Long, Sylvia, ill. II. Title.
PZ8.3.M393Bec 2007
[E]--dc22
2006032871

To Caroline,
the newest baby in our clan

—J.W.

To Amira Jean Long,
the mother of my grandchildren

—S.L.

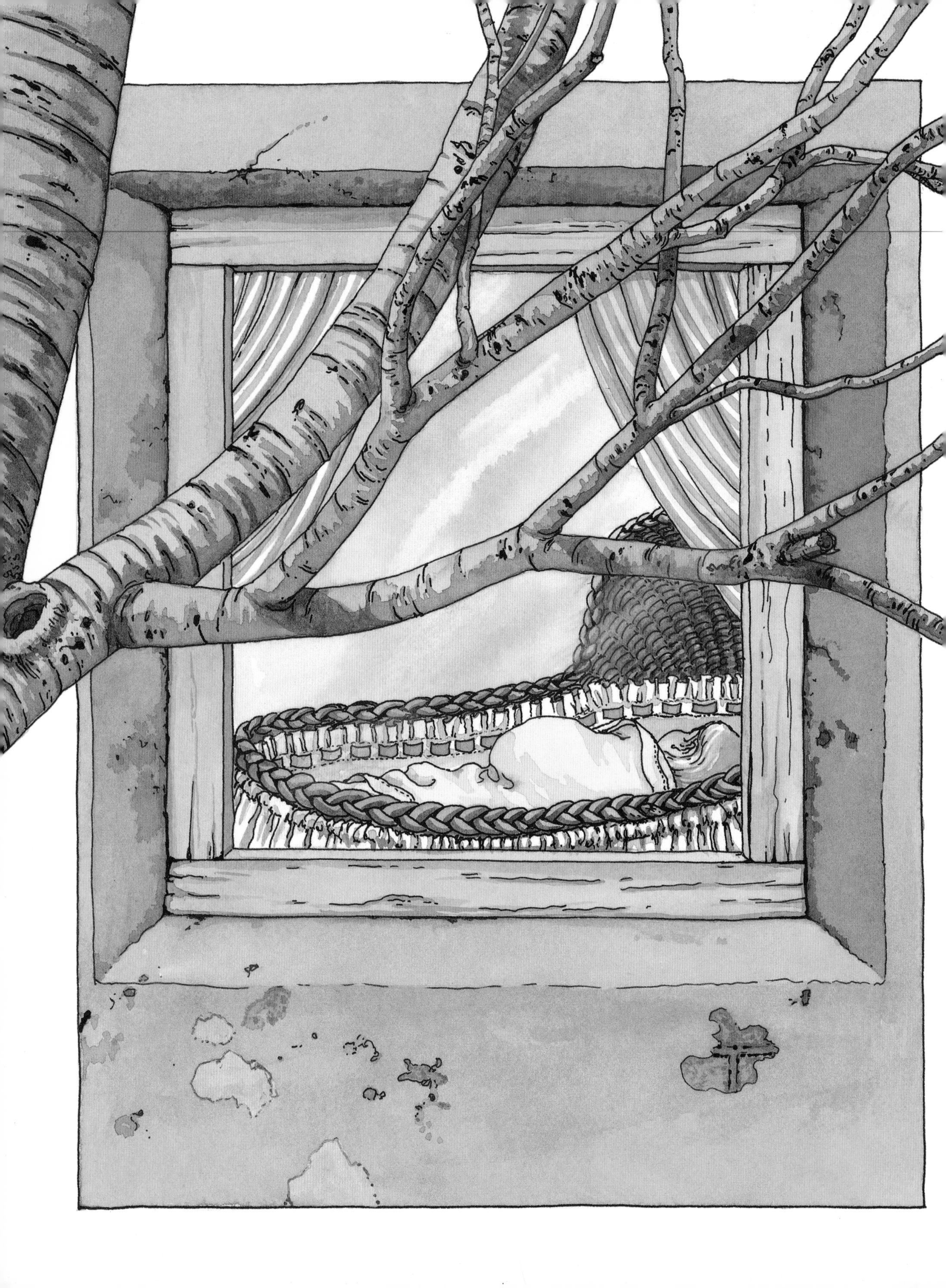

Because you are my baby...

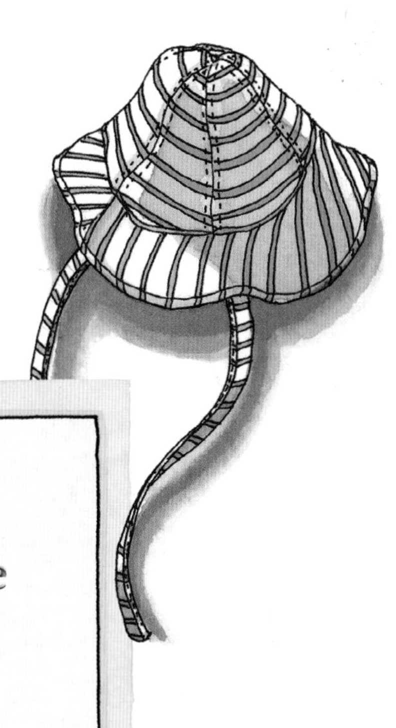

I'll find you shade
out in the sun,
for you're my
long-eared little one.

I'll teach you
how to dash and race,
place feathery kisses
on your face.

I'll walk a line
for you to follow,
snuggle with you
in our hollow.

I'll trot with care to keep you near,
grunt words of comfort in your ear.

I'll show you
flowers soft and sweet,
so you will know
just where to eat.

I'll watch you closely
while you play,
from morning's light
'til end of day.

Together we'll play hide and seek,
through desert grasses tall and sleek.

I'll hug you tight
beneath my wing
and teach you how
to chirp and sing.

I'll gather twigs
and make a nest,
the perfect place
for you to rest.

I'll show you how to bounce and leap,
purr lullabies to help you sleep.

I'll keep you snug
within our boot,
and teach you when
to *whoo* and *hoot*.

I'll sing you moon songs through the night,
where shadows play in milky light.

I'll teach you
everything I know
and guide you
as you learn and grow...

...because you are
my baby.